THROUGH WILD LENSES

A THRILLOGY OF SHORT HORROR STORIES

RED QUEEN

DR. HERTZOG'S BLUE HEAVEN

ROSE GOLD OBSESSION

MARGY LANG

ISBN's 978-0-9823197-3-4
0-9823197-3-8

Library of Congress Cataloging-in-Publication Data has been applied for.

Published by Sportive Marketing, Inc.
P.O. Box 24570, Jacksonville Florida, 32441, U.S.A.

margy@sportive-marketing.com

Table of Contents

THE LENS

There is a story to be told from most observations.
Sometimes we need a prompt to record our stories.
My prompt was a string of nightmares.
It helps to record your dreams and nightmares.
You never know when you'll use the material.
At the conclusion of the stories are resources and drink pairings.
Armed with knowledge and refreshment, read on.

RED QUEEN

Teeccino, a triple bottom line company, resonated more with her growing sustainability practice, but in a pinch Myrrdian drank a Panera coffee, black. Maybe the caffeine would balance the rawness of the Cextone Corporation job interview that had ended thirty-eight minutes prior.

While she had wanted to share her sustainability insights, the two interviewers and potential bosses were more interested in hearing about her unusual hobby. It was disturbing that they knew of her interests; she'd posted about the collection only in private forums.

Still, without hesitation the first interviewer had queried, "We understand you have a knife collection. Of all the things to collect, we didn't expect knives from a petite, young programmer. You must know what you're doing, eh?"

Initially, the question appeared both absurd and a violation of employment law. But it presented, as do many silly requests, an opportunity to share valuable knowledge.

"Actually, I collect daggers, not knives."

Their fascination piqued, one of them asked for clarification.

"A dagger, you know, is like a Bowie knife—a short, sharp blade, two cutting edges, and an unusually sharp point. Humans prefer daggers for close combat defense." Pausing to look at each man in turn, she continued. "Some popular models are the Pugio, the Corvo, and the Dirk. Medieval Roman daggers often had bling. You know, crystals or gemstones on the handles. Usually, you wear the sheath around your waist for readiness in close combat. The Dirk is a long, thrusting dagger." She stabbed the air, illustrating the correct way to handle a Dirk. "Scotsmen used it to defend themselves at sea. It's also good for close combat. I've heard it requires less strength to penetrate the organs than a Corvo." Noting their rapt attention, she said, "The Corvo is originally from Chile. Farmers used the dagger to harvest crops. When summoned for military duty, they took their Corvo. It has a special hook with a long, slender body. Today it's used by the Special Forces."

With that remark, the interviewers glanced at each other. One shuffled some forms in front of him.

The other cleared his throat and said, "Well, thank you for the information. You are a dagger expert. Can you tell us about your knowledge of our work on instrumentation for the aerospace industry?"

At the end of the hour-long interview, the men deemed Myrrdian a "good fit" and a knowledgeable "asset." They would recommend she be "brought on board to fix a few key issues." If the interview was successful, she expected to be hired to mop up the mess and then be disposed of like a soiled paper towel. But that was the nature of project-based work. Not exactly what Myrrdian wanted, knowing she was more than a fix-it technician. But in a tight job market, she had few choices. If the job were offered, the decision would be to either suck it up and produce solutions or make a big stink about the rotten culture. Not wanting to miss the opportunity for experience, she found the choice easy.

Less impressive to the interviewers was Myrrdian's disciple-like following of contemporary leadership theory. Without citing case studies and white papers, she had chosen to describe her project management style in simple terms: "It is akin to a Dirk—a thin dagger, but extended, with a twist at the inflection point."

The two men had excused themselves from the conference room.

Myrrdian mused as she waited: The Dirk could harvest those dead-headed interviewers, easily slicing off their body fat.

Cextone Corp. suddenly seemed tasty and dreamy and dripping with possibilities. Relishing the thought, she moved her index finger along the outline of the handle of the Pugio strapped to her thigh. Pushing the point into its thin sheath, she hummed the first verse of "My Kentucky Home." The song helped appease the blood-curdling battle cries in her head. The Pugio and "My Kentucky Home" were besties.

Leaving the interview after one of the guys said H.R. would call with a decision, Myrrdian craved comfort food. Googling the nearest Panera, she was soon delighted to find the café nearly empty. Settling in at a table for two, she impatiently waited for her charred chicken salad while sipping black coffee. Scrolling emails to distract herself from replaying the interview, she rocked gently in the hardwood chair. The latest *Stanford Graduate School of Business* e-newsletter caught her eye. Clicking on the article

"Rethink Competition in the Workforce," the hopeful soon-to-be project manager and middleware lover read the subtitle: "Great leaders often pit co-workers against each other to create a competitive atmosphere to drive outcomes."

The prospect of building battalions of workgroups, squashing competitors, and pitting employees in internal skirmishes made her giddy. When Myrrdian picked up her food at the counter, the server smiled back at her warmly. Eager to finish the article, Myrrdian hurried to her table.

"Though we'd love it if competition always had positive consequences, it often has a very negative consequence, both for the human condition and for the behavior of humans who live in fear of seeming to be a failure," said William P. Barnett, a contributor to the article, who also had coined the outcome, the *Red Queen consequence.*

While eating without intention, Myrrdian couldn't believe what she'd read. Not only did Barnett's words resonate, but the app Myrrdian was developing was titled *Red Queen Arising.* She skimmed the remainder of the article but read aloud the last sentence, a quote by Barnett cautioning companies to manage advances in technology: "Today's innovation is tomorrow's noose."

With those words, she sank into her chair, wondering if Cextone understood the complexities and processes to overthrow the competition. Myrrdian dearly wanted to head the battle cry, wielding a double-edged dagger. Her thoughts were interrupted by the buzzing of her cell phone.

Brenda, Cextone's human resources director, called with the job offer. Jubilantly, Myrrdian lifted the basket of toasted pita bread as if she had won Wimbledon and was hoisting the silver-plated Venus Rosewater Dish trophy for a crowd of raucous fans. An elderly couple at a small table in the corner near the restrooms gave her a thumbs-up and big smiles. After texting her mother with the news, Myrrdian ordered a mint dark chocolate chip cookie to go.

DAY ONE

Settling into a beige plastic chair at an empty table for four in Cextone's break room, Myrrdian opened the insulated Vera Wang satchel to unpack her lunch. The latest issue of *Popular Science* remained tucked under her arm. A pang of regret surfaced on the decision to bring the magazine to lunch. Not precisely a hipster move, but she thought it could be a conversation starter with her male co-workers. Plus, she was eager to read an article on A.I. used in drone parades. Placing the magazine face down on the corner of the table, she dug into her salad. The break from first-day-on-the-job jitters was welcomed ... until a woman in her early thirties, sporting a bright blue, long-sleeved dress and a string of blue-tinted freshwater pearls, entered the room.

Erica, the civic engagement officer (CEO) of Cextone, made a beeline for the occupied table, promptly plopping down before asking if she could join the new employee. Erica wasted no time divulging "executive secrets." During the executive committee meeting that morning, Erica shared, the human resources director had announced Myrrdian's hire, noting, "The woman has a penchant for collecting knives." Erica further divulged that the HR director had commented, "Not exactly what we expected. We thought she might be more a Hallmark ornament collector." The manager of Cextone's manufacturing division rebuked the comment, saying, "Thank God we hired someone interesting. Maybe she'll fire up the troops to get more work out of those lame numbskull developers." Hesitantly, Erica again shared comments from the HR director: "I thought she'd join the Zumba class, 'cause they're always looking to shed extra pounds. Instead, she wants to try ballroom dancing. Who'da thunk? I can't read 'em the way I used to."

Myrrdian paused her fork in midair, asking, "I guess you have a profile for every employee, huh?" to which Erica quickly dismissed the question with, "Oh, honey, we only talk about you if you are valuable."

Myrrdian's little smile masked her disappointment in Cextone's management team. Their remarks were hurtful and teetered on a violation of "dead lines" used in the military to mark enemy lines. A violation of the dead line carried a shoot-to-kill order.

"Back to the knife collection," Erica said. "Do you display them at home?"

Before Myrrdian could respond, she gestured to her mouthful of food. The new hire lightly touched the Pugio, straightened her back, the palm of her hand gently brushing the Glock tucked into her waistband. Myrrdian calculated that she could produce the gun with her left hand in less than five seconds while plunging the Pugio into Erica's shoulder. The blade would not just penetrate her shoulder but would significantly tear the muscle. In excruciating pain and horror, Erica would fall to the floor. A pistol whip to the neck would cripple but not kill the CEO.

Myrrdian took a deep gulp of air to gain her composure before leaning in. "I do have them on display," she replied. "No point in keeping them hidden. Ha-ha—no pun intended!" The pun, lost on Erica, made Myrrdian ask, laughingly, "Want me to describe them to you?"

The CEO quickly waved away the question and proceeded to complain that she wasn't paid what she was worth, yet managed to make more than "the geek-squad engineers." Snickering at her remark, she grunted and said, "It's rough, but someone without glasses and their hair parted on the side needs to be the face of the company."

In the distance, Myrrdian heard the rumble of a squadron. She listened intently for the scream of a battle cry, thinking it might have been the squeaking of Erica rubbing her patent leather shoes together. Spearing a slice of celery, the former soldier held it up, staring beyond it … at Erica's bloodshot eyeballs. The fork was a handy weapon. Few were instructed on how deadly it could be. The chorus of "My Kentucky Home" hummed softly in Myrrdian's head, and she eased the celery into her mouth. Tilting her head to one side as if intently listening to the CEO, Myrrdian heard the news of Erica's boyfriend's ability to renegotiate their monthly apartment rent, thereby allowing them to pay cash for their upcoming European vacation. The CEO reminded the new hire she could take only two weeks' holiday at a time, winked, and said, "Policy, you know," while raising her right hand and the index finger of her left hand, indicating she received six weeks' vacation.

Without hesitation, Erica whispered that her mother was battling breast cancer, which made the CEO feel guilty for planning a trip. "Not that I don't care about Mother's condition, but I think in six months she will be fine. We'll both need a break, and there is nothing you can do for someone going through treatments," she said, sighing as she cut a piece of chicken in the plastic container that looked like it once held a to-go order from the local Chinese restaurant.

Offering what she hoped was practical advice, Myrrdian suggested Erica run the plans by her family.

Vigorously shaking her head, Erica scolded her, saying, "You sound just like everyone else."

Myrrdian's attention focused on the bottom of her salad's plastic bowl. Thin layers of olive oil and Bragg Apple Cider Vinegar "With The Mother" surrounded a few herbs that had sifted through the arugula. The lunch break had evaporated; her lunch was not filling; the conversation was absurd; the *Popular Science* article was unread. She wanted to depart as quickly and unceremoniously as possible. Myrrdian excused herself, thanked the CEO, and grabbed at the periodical, causing it to slide onto the floor where it landed face up.

Erica looked down and blurted, "OMG! You read that? I thought *Popular Science* was long gone."

Quick to dispel the myth, Myrrdian picked up the magazine, pointing to the month and year of publication. "It's current, and it's a great way to kill a lunch break."

Not amused, Erica said, "You must be not only the first woman to collect knives, but the first woman I know who reads *Popular Science*. My sixth-grade science teacher used to bring it into class and point out these bizarro gadgets people had invented. Crazy stuff, right?"

The tipping point in leadership is tough to execute. It seems the middle managers and seasoned entry-level employees are relatively easy to handle. They show up and run the game plan. The fringes at the top and bottom rungs of the organization exert stress and sap resources. Tipping point leadership requires managing the extremes without draining valuable resources from other areas.

Settling herself onto her office chair, Myrrdian jiggled to find a spot ten or fifteen percent more comfortable. What if she never found a comfortable position? What if Cextone's health insurance changed and her counseling sessions were no longer covered? What if the career move was a grave mistake?

At the end of the workday, Myrrdian took the stairs, pausing long enough to survey the stairwell's pale green paint. The color reminded her of the V.A. outpatient clinic where she met once a week with her counselor. At their last meeting, before Myrrdian left for the job at Cextone, the counselor told her about a new treatment plan specific to women vets with PTSD who were returning to the workforce. Myrrdian was eager to get started with the new program, but now worried she might not find a counselor who was familiar with the treatment.

When leaving the building, Myrrdian determined that she'd greet every co-worker with a little smile, while eyeing them for their potential combat skills. Judging others and measuring things were lifelong pursuits. Her old man had wanted her to follow in his footsteps and be a math teacher. With no disrespect, she had laughed off the suggestion. Her intolerance for children plus an insatiable appetite for daggers would not add up to a successful career as a middle-school math teacher.

Inside her car, she smiled. First-day jitters had finally worn off. Starting the ignition also ignited a cumbersome flashback: dead lines. For days she had not thought about the circumstances surrounding the flashbacks, grateful for the respite from the panic attacks they produced. Still, the flashback made her grip the steering wheel until she summoned the song, placed her hand confidently on the Pugio, and took a deep breath.

In no rush to sit in an empty apartment, she stalled, checking her email. Her father's email, titled "Barrier-breaking math pioneer," aroused her curiosity. The article about Ingrid Daubechies, professor of math at Princeton and Duke, discussed wavelets and their applications across varied disciplines (the sciences, arts, etc.). He included a quote from Daubechies: "The atmosphere you need for those groups to feel appreciated is an atmosphere that will encourage creativity—just to be more open, to entertain a different way of looking at things."

That's Pops, thought Myrrdian, *always trying to feed me information related to my interests.* Before leaving the parking lot, she wrote to him that she would call in a few days.

To learn her way around the new city, Myrrdian decided to take a different route home from work. The practice would introduce her to new neighborhoods and make her more comfortable. Driving in a community of lookalike, two-story brick homes, she found the sameness bothersome. Her mind wandered to the vastness of wavelets, those mathematical building blocks that help gather data and uphold its integrity. She slowed down, immersed in the thought of how Cextone could build execution into strategy by using mathematical models! She laughed, thinking about childhood visits with her grandparents. In their best Lawrence Welk impression, together they would exclaim that their only granddaughter was "Wunnerful, wunnerful!"

The childhood memory prompted Myrrdian to pull in to a park close to her apartment. She recognized the sparsely furnished green space and thought it an excellent way to enjoy the last vestiges of sunlight streaming through leafy oak trees. Perched on a picnic table, she extracted a small journal from her jacket pocket. Her notes were written in pencil, allowing for multiple edits. Ink was too permanent for this project.

Turning the journal pages as if they were ancient sea scrolls, she stopped at the page listing persons who had influenced her job search and her move. Some had encouraged her, some begged her to stay, and some said they didn't care. In sum, the influencers had not helped her much. And it was time for a change. She erased two names: Pops and Mom. Swept away by a few vigorous strokes, they fell to the ground like dust from a saw blade.

Relations with her parents had strained under the weight of PTSD. Intimidated by Myrrdian's vibrancy and infatuation with weapons, they believed their child could maneuver life independently.

She cupped the small journal, holding it close to her mouth. A tear dropped onto the page where she'd made room for two more players. When identified, she'd enlist them, pit them against each other, and let them do battle until the winner survived and the loser died.

Red Queen Arising was far from the fairy-tale story of an *Alice in Wonderland* character. This game required brutal strength and cunning intelligence. The main character, Red Queen, dominated the pace and outcome, defending herself against warriors by chanting, "Don't call me up."

MY HEART

I pushed the keypad to gain entry to my apartment. I threw my knapsack on the kitchen counter, jumped onto the love seat and curled up, hugging a pillow before thinking about preparing a cup of chamomile tea. I don't remember how much tea I consumed before being jolted by the harsh ringing of the doorbell. Prying myself from the comfort of the couch, I looked at my Glock 17 sitting on the counter. It was too far for me to reach.

Forgoing my reinforcement, I stood facing the door, and sheepishly asked, "Who is it?"

The deep-sounding but muted response came from what I determined to be a young man, maybe six feet tall. "Delivery from Al's Pizza."

I barked back, "I didn't order a pizza."

He mumbled, "Compliments of Cextone Corporation."

It seemed surreal (or was it unreal) that a company would deliver pizza to a new hire. In an annoyed tone, I said, "Leave it on the floor."

"Sure thing," he replied, and walked down the hallway to the elevator.

Waiting to hear the elevator doors open, I then grabbed the Glock before timidly opening the apartment door to retrieve the box. I placed it on the coffee table and pulled the top up. A waft of steaming veggies greeted me. Puzzled, I tried to recall if I had mentioned I practiced "meatless Mondays" to HR or the CEO or my workgroup.

As I reached for a slice of pie, my cell phone rang. It was Brenda, the human resources director.

"Hello, Myrrdian. I just wanted to check on you. I'm two blocks away. Okay to swing by?"

With some trepidation, I curtly replied, "Yes, of course." I placed the Glock in the top drawer of the nearby cabinet.

Brenda pleasantly announced herself as the "Welcome Wagon" and entered the living room, chatting about the nearby yoga studio. The conversation took an abrupt turn when she stumbled on expressing remorse for the remarks about me to Cextone's executive team.

Not wanting to linger on the subject, I shrugged and replied in a soft voice, "It happens. Much too often."

She apologized again and began pleading for me to keep quiet about the remarks. If I agreed to be silent, Brenda promised to support my aspiration to advance quickly at Cextone. Wanting to lock eyes, I couldn't; her eyes darted like spooked fish.

Abruptly, I stopped the plea by putting up a hand and exclaiming, "Let it go already!"

Her head dropped. She knew she was exposed and desperate.

I'd make this as painless as possible and broke the room's silence. "Would you like a slice of the pizza you ordered to be delivered here?"

"What pizza?"

I was opening the kitchen drawer to retrieve forks and knives while Brenda wondered aloud who had ordered the pizza. She stated sarcastically, "Maybe it was your friend, the CEO, Erica."

Lying in the drawer, dark and handsomely muscular, my Glock beckoned. In a mere second I moved to retrieve the Glock, spin around gracefully like a ballerina, and aim the loaded gun at Brenda's forehead. Opening her mouth to scream while raising her arms, Brenda seemed to offer a welcoming expression to the speeding bullet invading her face just above the nose. Its entry stopped dead a scream and a life. Blood and tiny bits of tissue spewed forth from the back of her head, spraying the white door she was still leaning against, giving it a texture of an abstract painting. Brenda slid into a heap on the floor. Moving an arm out of the way, I felt her neck, then her wrist for a pulse.

Taking a shawl from the sofa, I unceremoniously draped it over Brenda's shoulders and wrapped her bleeding head. Then I hung my head. Words from the song "Absence" came to mind. Snuggling the gun to my ear, I leaned on the kitchen counter. The kill had been anticlimactic. The golden-brown skin of my neck felt sickly damp. A wave of unconsciousness swept over me as a flash of jagged pain blurred my vision. Squinting hard, I opened my eyes to see a slice of pizza missing from the box. And the thin wax paper liner under the pizza slices had dark streaks. Lifting the pizza revealed smeared words written with a marker on the wax paper. After some studying, I read the letters: *I know where you live, honey.*

Adding to the chaos, the doorbell rang again.

Walking rapidly to the peephole, I saw a dark-haired, hooded man. Inches separated us. I hollered, "What?"

One eye zoomed squarely into the eyehole … he had an uncanny resemblance to Mark, my former boyfriend.

In a voice familiar to me, he replied, "I delivered a pizza not long ago and made a mistake. I have a replacement pizza."

By the time he'd finished, I knew I had to be stern. "I'm busy. You can't just show up out of the blue, Mark."

Jiggling the door handle, he threatened to break the lock. He kicked at the door. Not wanting to alert the neighbors, I opened the door, revealing Mark dressed in a black golf shirt and khaki pants, with a baseball cap emblazoned with the pizza shop's name.

The blood-curdling screams of villagers outside the encampment grew so loud I couldn't hear "My Kentucky Home." How dare he follow me to this city!

Another cry arose from the field, not a hundred yards from the dead line. It sounded like a young boy.

Mark strode into the apartment and bumped me slightly since his head was oddly turned to the left. The angle blocked him from seeing Brenda's body dabbled with red blotches, a small hole in her forehead and liquids oozing from orifices.

Like an actor walking onto a stage, Mark stood firmly in the middle of the living room and raised his head slightly, reciting, "I want you. Without you, my life is nothing. You are my everything. Honey, I can't live without you." He gestured with his hands as if to hug the air and continued. "I can't stand the loneliness. I can't stand life when I don't speak to you day and night."

Snapping back, I challenged his way of showing me love—by stalking me, being creepy, deceitful.

My response made him turn his head to the right. His eyes widened. "My God!" he exclaimed. "What happened to Brenda?"

Not wanting to waste time sharing details, I said, "Brenda made you do this, didn't she? She is the enemy, and you confided in her. Then she asked you for help, and because you fell in love with her, you've come to kill me. So, here!"

Retrieving the Glock, I presented it to Mark atop my flattened palm, like a plate of appetizers. I asked him to take it, use it to kill me, and explain why he committed a double murder.

In a pleading voice, he replied, "I didn't kill her, and I'm not killing you."

Slowly, I raised my flattened hand and grasped the gun, pushing it into my right breast, sliding it over my heart, inching it up to the base of my neck. Holding the pistol at an angle, I stared at Mark with my best poker face.

Mark begged me to stop while putting his hand over mine as if to cover the gun. The force of his gripping hand twisted my wrist and fingers, igniting the bullet in the chamber. The slender silver bullet with its brownish copper-colored cap shuttled down the smooth cylinder, becoming airborne as it sped towards its target. The bullet entered Mark's chest, cleanly. There it traveled at lightning speed, barely careening off a vertebra while shredding nerves, muscle, and tissue in its tracks like a four-wheeler on a deserted road. Instead of dust and dirt kicking up in its wake, waves of blood filled the holes, crevices, and punctures.

Stumbling, Mark leaned to his left, swayed backward, and fell into Brenda's lap, his body superimposed onto hers. The pair looked like an ice-skating duo finishing their choreographed dance by collapsing on the ice.

Stunned by the gun going off in my hand, I stepped back, reviewing the scene. A rush of panic and fear covered me in a roughly sewn cape as I yelled, "What did you do!"

Mark gasped and squeezed his eyes tightly, unable to move to inspect his crippled chest cavity. Dying gave him a gray appearance. I noticed a frothy spit of blood collected on Brenda's blouse from his mouth. Her eyeballs appeared to be covered in a film of Vaseline.

Mark exited the game. Never much of a fighter, he'd racked up the losses. He sucked at everything … Scrabble, poker, esports, shooting hoops in the driveway. I wished I had set up dead lines to eliminate him without having to endure all the sulking and excuses when he crossed those lines.

He had made every simple situation a tangled mess—like ending his life in the company of Brenda. The thought of them entering heaven together was freakish and hurtful. Taking a step back from the merged bodies, I swished the saliva in my mouth and spat on the corpses to douse the last flicker of life.

Pulling the Pugio from the sheath strapped to my thigh, I held it up to the light and let the dusky light kiss it every so lightly before I, too, kissed the high-carbon steel. I then offered final words before the carving.

Goodbye, comrades. You'll never know the game of Red Queen Arising. I'll never have the privilege of whipping your butts and teaching you right from wrong. Instead, you'll perish in a stagnant pond and be eaten by bottom dwellers.

DEAD LINES

A hard rap on the door in unison with the doorbell's shrieking roused Myrrdian. She looked down at her cell phone lying on her stomach, and her hands folded as if in prayer. A second rap on the door made her blink hard while tossing the blanket off her legs.

A high-pitched voice sliced through what was left of the silence now dripping from the apartment walls: "Hey, girl. It's Brenda. You home? Are you okay? I brought you next month's schedule of yoga classes."

Swinging her legs off the couch, Myrrdian stepped onto the cool hardwood floor, squarely facing the wall which proudly displayed her latest oil painting, *The Red Queen's Heart*. Written across the bottom of the canvas with a gold-colored Sharpie was a quote from Robert Ludlum: "Hope is the only thing stronger than fear."

While Myrrdian was deployed, a fellow soldier had shared the quote with her. His girlfriend had sent it to him to squelch his fears during night watch of the dead lines encircling the encampment. Trip wires triggered an alarm if anything or anyone crossed the lines. The soldier on duty was required to shoot to kill—stray animals, enemy soldiers, or villagers setting off the alarm. Myrrdian sensed the soldier was fearful of the assignment but more fearful he would never see his girlfriend again.

"Hope is the only thing stronger than fear" became a mantra for Myrrdian, in her attempts to soothe the cruel reality of being discharged from duty with withered and torn emotional scars. However, the mantra wasn't enough to dismiss the flashbacks and emotional illness. Counseling helped some. A counselor helped Myrrdian ward off some of the primeval screams; she learned the words to "My Kentucky Home." But she needed more than a song to fight off PTSD, she needed strength. Evidence of the kills lingered … white walls and a floor sprinkled with blood like a painter had carelessly flung his brush; a bucket of heavy kitchen towels floating in pink-colored Clorox; stained Handi Wipes lying exhausted at the bottom of the compact washer in the living room closet.

Brenda would be proud to know she'd died in Mark's arms. She admired him even though she had said she never met him. Mark was at peace. His clamoring for Myrrdian's attention had ended.

Myrrdian looked away from *The Red Queen's Heart*, the red, black, and yellow abstract, and a soft smile caressed her lips before she saw, on the floor, the small black journal sprawled in front of the painting. They were lone visitors in a cavernous gallery, challenged by how abstract art inspires the brain to view things differently. The code written for the Red Queen Arising game was an intersection of abstract and competition using A.I. The action took place in several famous galleries. Despite the expected criticism from veteran gamers, developers, and skeptics, Myrrdian felt a deep sense of accomplishment in the project. Long ago, she had shed the notion that women couldn't produce games populated with priestings running around madly to pursue domination while avoiding dead lines.

Taking the final steps to unlock the door, she leaned over the kitchen counter with an outstretched arm to reach the Glock, and mustered a friendly reply: "Be right there."

A Dream Within a Dream
by Edgar Allan Poe
Take this kiss upon your brow!
And, in parting from you now,
Thus, much let me avow—
You are not wrong, who deem
That my days have been a dream;
Yet if hope has flown away
In a night, or in a day,
In a vision, or in none,
Is it therefore the less gone?
All that we see or seem
Is but a dream within a dream.

DR. HERTZOG'S BLUE HEAVEN

A thin layer of ground haze held the remaining silence of early dawn. It was 6:00 AM, and the only occupant of the three-story red-brick building was holed up in his office, a converted walk-in closet with a small table and chair, PC, microwave, and sparse inventory of office supplies. Thomas, the janitor, was quietly speaking into his cell phone, occasionally scribbling notes in his three-ring spiral notebook.

I often thought the hour before this mysteriously quiet man clocked in was spent reading the local newspaper's Sports page or picking numbers for that night's lottery drawing. Or maybe he was meditating or praying.

Whatever he was doing, I was sure he was sipping on a large coffee from the 7-Eleven store located next to the office. Upon my entering the building's side entrance, the cheap Columbian coffee waft greeted me. The acidic aroma lingered in the hallway, following me into the stairwell.

On occasion, I'd hear Thomas's office door open after the stairwell door shut. The first time I heard it, I thought the noise came from the fireproof stairwell door's hinges. The next time I heard it, I stopped my climb up the steps, listening for his footsteps. It was like we were cowboys in a shootout in an empty field, waiting for someone to make the first move. I never heard his footsteps in the hallway, nor the closing of his office door. Maybe the janitor made sure it was an employee who had entered the building and not an intruder. Or perhaps he wanted to make sure I kept moving up the steps to the third-floor laboratory. A few times, I wanted to rap on his office door to surprise him and let him know I knew he was observing my moves, but I thought it best to leave him to his business.

Always punctual, Dr. Alfred Hertzog, the lead chemist at the pharmaceutical company, arrived at 6:45 AM, in his 1969 horizon blue 280 Mercedes-Benz SL Roadster with parchment-colored leather interior. The car was a showcase of sleek design and mechanical wonder. It was his pride and joy, and he parked it in the far reaches of the employee parking lot to avoid being marred by dust or curious co-workers. The walk to the building's side door taxed Dr. Hertzog's body enough that his wheezing preempted his arrival on the third floor. Chugging along and letting off steam with big sighs, he mirrored the car's mechanics: precision gearwork and a belch when accelerating uphill.

His daily wardrobe matched the palette of his treasured vehicle. Hertzog wore dark or light blue golf shirts from late spring into late fall—either a long-sleeved dark blue Izod or a light blue dress shirt with a white undershirt in the winter. The chemist needed no jacket or overcoat but did carry an umbrella, even on partially cloudy days. The umbrella served as a cane to assist his beleaguered knees. My guess is his pride prevented him from using a cane. The pride he took in outworking others and his profound research appeared to be rooted in his Germanic heritage. Alfred Hertzog was courageous, from his work ethic to sturdy conduct, never shying from complex projects. He successfully managed a diverse band of scientists on the quest to produce a drug to combat the deadliest of diseases.

Considered a loner, Hertzog shielded his private life, never commenting about family or friends. At a Monday morning staff meeting, while we waited for a tardy project director, a lab technician mentioned he and his fiancée had visited the Holocaust Museum in Washington, DC, over the weekend. He described the depository as informative, moving, and sad. He glanced across the conference room table at Dr. Hertzog to see his response. He lifted his eyes from the memo he was reading and then dropped his head as if burying it in his thick neck and broad shoulders.

Poor man, I thought. Someone needs to tell him he's not responsible for anything past generations might have done or experienced.

This morning as Dr. Hertzog walked to his corner office, he stopped at my glass-walled cubicle, propping his body against the half-wall. His umbrella sturdily held him in place. "Good morning, Miss Cartwright. I can only assume your day has started well," he said, annunciating every syllable succinctly to allow for small breaths between the words.

"Indeed, Dr. Hertzog." With a deep voice containing a smile, I added, "I've started blending the magic elixir of Dr. Frankenstein, exactly as prescribed."

Hertzog's eyes lightened. "As expected, I will review the formula. I hope we've got it this time, Miss Cartwright."

Not wanting to fall prey to trite humor when discussing work, we locked eyes briefly. His steel-blue oculus organs matched his shirt, his car, and the temporary color of skin tainted by the drug's activation sequence. The driven scientist tapped the tip of his umbrella on the nondescript brown-patterned carpet, pivoted toward the hallway, and instructed, "Keep your foot on the pedal, Miss Cartwright."

The experimental drug's toxicity could kill lab mice with a drop placed on a cotton swab inserted into a nostril. Chemists, who followed Hertzog's work, respected the drug's powers to cure and to destroy. Lengthy protocols and elaborate security measures slowed the pace of work. It felt like the drug might never be approved for human testing.

To protect scientists and lab technicians, Hertzog had formulated the drug with an ingenious safety net. The formula ignited its poisonous powers only when initiated by a chemical chain stoked by an acidic derivative in thermal conditions. The drug killed radical cells and the ability to induce cardiac arrest. It had taken over three years for Hertzog to discover how to protect it from self-igniting in the lab rat's harsh gastronomical juices. If the drug were approved for clinical trials, it could save hundreds of thousands of lives. Fallen into the wrong hands, it could be used for criminal activity.

Approval of the drug would be the capstone achievement to Hertzog's fulfilling career. For me, it meant seniority in the company's male-dominated organization.

Four months later, the leaves were ablaze with brilliant coloration, and we were in the middle of a particularly lengthy testing phase. It surprised me when I was summoned by Dr. Hertzog, to meet in the small conference room. Upon my entering the drab room, Hertzog pointed to a chair. Heeding his silent command, I sat and squirmed a bit.

"The purpose of this impromptu meeting," he stated while leaning against a whiteboard, "is an inquiry."

The meeting was significant; Hertzog referred to inquiries as "mapping out a scientific journey."

With a softer than usual tone, he asked, "Do you know why Thomas is arriving off-schedule, as late as seven-fifteen some mornings?"

Caught off guard by the subject, I hurriedly answered, "I heard Thomas was having tests done for a health condition."

Hertzog shook his head as if he already had that information and then told me Thomas had met him several times in the parking lot and shared his diagnosis of an incurable disease. Distraught by the inevitableness, Thomas was unsure how to tell his wife and son of the outcome. Hertzog suggested he lie to his family by telling them he had been diagnosed with severe heart disease. Thomas's wife and son would accept heart disease instead of the rigorous and treacherous death brought on by the incurable disease.

"Seems reasonable" is all I could muster, stumbling on the news and dumbfounded that a janitor would confide in an astute scientist who presented scientific papers at international conferences.

In a flash I recalled the staff meeting and the mention of the Holocaust Museum. Gazing at Hertzog's face, I perceived his sternness to have crumbled on the edges, like his favorite raspberry streusel muffin.

ANOTHER CHILLY MORNING

A week later, a damp chill in the morning air snapped its fingers at my face as I left my car and walked the short distance to the side door. We were to meet at 6:00 AM. My teeth chattered, and my heart raced as I approached Thomas, slumped over slightly as he leaned against the cold red-brick wall. The white ghostliness of his skin matched the large white Styrofoam cup of 7-Eleven coffee. He tipped his Mets baseball cap to me. Then we stood in silence.

I held my breath as long as I could, not wanting to smell the coffee. I covered my mouth with my hand. Thomas looked over at me, shook his head, and raised the cup a bit as if offering me a sip.

The whole scene dripped with anxiety. I wanted to hold my nose or cough or vomit. Hertzog arrived, greeting us with a nod, and proceeded to unlock the door and disarm the security system.

He ushered us into the dark hall, instructing Thomas, "Turn on the lights and put your lunch in the refrigerator and get the morning paper. We'll meet you in twenty minutes. Heat your coffee in the microwave in a mug, but don't let it boil."

Twenty minutes later, Dr. Hertzog and I stood outside the men's restroom on the first floor. Dr. Hertzog knocked on the door and announced us. I instantly felt uneasy. It's not every day a young woman enters a men's restroom occupied by a co-worker and her boss. On the ride down in the elevator from the third floor, Hertzog had been quiet until the elevator touched the first floor.

Before stepping out, he turned and stated, "Laboratories are not antiseptic, white-walled sanctuaries."

Entering the men's restroom, I quickly looked beyond the urinals to the lineup of three private stalls. Hertzog rapped the knuckle of his index finger at the center of the first stall's walnut door. Thomas gingerly opened the door, holding it with his left hand. A nondescript beige mug sat precariously on top of the toilet paper dispenser. The morning's newspaper sat at Thomas's feet, opened to the Sports page and the previous night's box scores.

Embarrassingly, Thomas tugged on his shirttail to cover his private parts and pulled the waistband of his pants to hike them up, covering his bare knees. I asked him for the mug and tested the temperature of the coffee with a thermometer. I was determined not to look again at Thomas's naked thighs. Instead, I focused on his full head of black hair sprinkled with gray streaks, neatly parted. His sideburns looked recently trimmed. *How dignified,* I thought.

Hertzog fished for the vial in the front pocket of his baggy khakis. In one motion, he poured the clear liquid from the vial into the mug. The potion immediately produced a milky foam.

The laboratory, offices, and hallways turned painfully silent by midday. Even Hertzog's wheezing seemed muffled as he paced the halls. Remarks by co-workers identified Thomas a "quiet and righteous man" and a "rabid Mets fan." A couple of guys in the break room commented that Thomas had once told him he went to Mets games mostly because he craved the juicy jumbo hot dogs slathered with gooey cheese sauce and an extra dose of relish.

Another co-worker, trying to be a good scientist, explained the cause of Thomas's demise: "Poor fella must have been taking a dump. They tell you not to strain. That's why so many people die on the john."

Another reported overhearing the administrative assistant to the HR director sharing that Thomas's body had bluish slate coloring around his bulbous nose, nostril, and lips.

Without hesitation, the human resources department sent a staff person to gather Thomas's personal belongings from his locker and a small desk that resembled a computer stand. Thomas referred to the stand as his desk, kidding his family of having a "desk job."

Unaware of Thomas's habits, the human resources staff person didn't retrieve his uneaten lunch stored in his mini-refrigerator. Thomas had purchased the dorm-sized refrigerator to prevent having to mingle with the scientists in the lunchroom. The new janitor would make the unpleasant discovery of the rotted lunch. Thomas once told one of the young technicians his wife always packed his lunch with leftovers from the previous night's dinner. Some staff wondered if the mini-fridge could be moved to the third-floor break room.

Thomas's replacement would bring his or her own set of quirks, style, and demeanor. Hopefully, their coffee would be in a sealed thermos bottle. Then the acrid odor would be contained and wouldn't escape under the door, prance along the hallway, and slither like a snake into the stairwell.

It didn't take too long before my nightmares set in, along with an overwhelming feeling of remorse. There was no one to discuss my mental anguish. Every counselor, shrink, and a friend would want to know the backstory.

A LONG ROAD

The next day, Dr. Hertzog called in sick. He reminded me to distribute the weekly memo to the project team, with updates from the FDA on the drug's beta testing schedule. He ended the phone message with, "Miss Cartwright … it is with great anticipation that we move forward … confident in the formula's applicability."

I listened to the message again, detecting a clicking sound. It sounded like the shifting of car gears. Perhaps Dr. Hertzog was not sick but was taking a road trip.

Accompanied by the songs of Il Devo, Hertzog turned up the volume of the CD. He wanted to suppress the echoes in his brain of Thomas's wife's screams after the researcher had called her with the news of her husband's untimely death. Alfred hoped, in time, the cries would subside. But Thomas's legacy would live on.

With only a cellphone, Internet connection, and the old PC assigned to the janitor, Thomas resourcefully sold patented formulas and test results to a ring of info-tech thieves. The information was shared with data brokers in Libya. Monies paid to Thomas for the specs handsomely supplemented the janitor's hourly wage.

Judiciously, Thomas earmarked the monies for family expenses. The only visible splurge was two season tickets to the Mets games. The funds were deposited into an account in small increments. One account was to fund his son's college tuition, and another made automatic payments for a whole life insurance policy. He wanted to make sure his wife would never work full-time or have to sell their modest home to pay for living expenses.

Once the monies started flowing, Thomas reflected on how lucky he was to sell the intellectual property and scientific notes. A cohort in the operation spoke with Thomas about what kind of information was needed and warned Thomas things could change rapidly, stating, "It's not falling into an opportunity, Thomas, it is falling into a trap. When the money comes in, and you get used to it, you'll be addicted. Think about your life when money dries up."

FBI investigators escalated the investigation because of the international threat precipitated by the drug's capability as a weapon of mass destruction. They named the case "Double Dose." On occasion, FBI agents disguised as Food and Drug Administration (FDA) officials met with Hertzog in his office. They indicated they were close to gathering enough evidence to arrest Thomas. Hertzog moved quickly to avoid Thomas being charged. The bad publicity would hinder the FDA's approval and mar the company's next round of investor money.

SPARKY'S PLACE

Settling himself into the Roadster's soft leather seat, he dropped his shoulders while straightening his neck. He cleared his voice to address God. Alfred spoke meekly: "It was mutually agreed upon, right? I beg for your mercy and forgiveness." Alfred waited in silence for a response.

The drive became monotonous; one farm looked like the next. Rounding a bend, he passed a pub with outdoor seating and quickly made a three-point U-turn. Pulling into Sparky's Place, he noted it appeared to be part bar, part grille, and part dive. Inside the run-down establishment, he looked around but saw no one but a small man with a neatly trimmed mustache and long sideburns.

You must be Sparky. And I'm Dr. Alfred Hertzog.

The man standing behind the bar smiled briefly before answering. Yes, sir, nice to meet you. You must be thirsty after the drive, and well, yesterday's events.

Taken aback by Sparky's reference to "yesterday's events," Hertzog snapped, What are you referencing? You don't know me. I only came in for a Negroni—one part gin, one part vermouth, and one part Campari. Stirred, not shaken, plenty of ice, and a twist of lime.

Right. I'll get the Negroni in no time flat. But so that you know, your deed yesterday ... it was big news round here.

And what do you call this part of the country?

Why, this is Blue Heaven, Dr. Hertzog! A special place for special people who've done special acts.

Special, huh? Can you give me an example of something special?

Sure thing. But taste that Negroni first. Let me know if it's up to par.

Yes, it's quite good, thank you. But your comment perturbs me.

Okay, then. Do you want to know what people have done to get themselves here? I'll tell you what I did. Just so you know upfront, Doc. I couldn't help myself. My mind wasn't mine. I'm sure the devil himself possessed me.

Go on. This ought to be interesting.

I blew up a young man into a hundred pieces. First, I held the rifle up to his belly, hard, and then I pumped it. When I rolled him over, I saw a twinkle in his one eye. So I held my rifle to his cheek, pressed hard, and pressed again and again until he was nearly beheaded. Then I took the shovel lying up against the barn door, and I dug a hole in his lower belly, deep, scraping whatever guts I could onto the ground.

Jesus, man. How can you be running a bar? You should be behind bars.

Funny one, Doc. I murdered that young boy because he raped my daughter and got her pregnant. She was a young thing, a damn good basketball player. When he was done knockin up my daughter, he coerced her teammate and ended up raping her. No father wants to see his daughter hurt. And no father should have to see his daughter die during childbirth. You being a scientist, you know the order of life and death. I shouldn't have to bury my daughter and her daughter. My wife and I had the two buried in the same grave.

That young boy caused our town grief, and my actions caused my family even more suffering. So I took my life. I double-bagged my face and neck so my wife wouldn't see the hole in my head. I pinned a note to my boot, telling her I loved her.

God was angry with me, Doc. He fussed at me, yelling at me as He leaned over the side of this place that looked like a canyon. He was so close. I tried to reach Him with my outstretched hand, but He backed away. But He's a merciful one. Got me to Blue Heaven. Not exactly utopia here, but it sure beats Hell!

You can't tell me this is a purgatory or a spiritual place where you live and work in your afterlife?

That is precisely what it is! But Blue Heaven is not like the song. We've all committed horrific acts, but we are a remorseful bunch. We don't have any personal agendas, hidden truths, deceit, or contempt. We left all that behind when we killed our souls. So we're clean. We're content.

It's hard for me to follow your logic, Sparky. It still doesn't make sense.

Look, Alfred. You are visiting Blue Heaven, which means things are not looking too great for you. You don't get here unless you're deader than a doornail.

You are a fine actor, Sparky, for this little stage you call a pub.

Ha, Alfred. I tell you, you are the actor, hiding your life behind the goals of your work. In Blue Heaven, we work, but we also care deeply for the other souls. They freaked out, hurt themselves, and hurt others, but they didn't mean to inflict so much pain.

Indeed, God would not let a person deliberately harm another person and then commit them to a comfortable community like Blue Heaven.

When you are temporarily disabled, and your actions don't match your mindset, your soul does not live in the depths of hatred and fear known as Hell. You suffer enough every day in remorse for your actions. Our God is a God of mercy. Thus, there is a Blue Heaven.

It is scientifically impossible for a place to coexist in two states—Earth and Blue Heaven. You must be a spirit. Or maybe you're related to Casper the Ghost! I'm puzzled, so I'm leaving. But before I go, if I'm following your grandiose tale correctly, everyone in Blue Heaven killed themselves?

Doc, not everyone wrapped their head in duct tape, covered it with a bag, stuck a pistol in their mouth, and pulled the trigger. Some lived for years in horrific emotional conditions and never sought help. So, in a sense, they did kill themselves. Some showed up like me, with half a face and someone's blood on them. If there were no Blue Heaven, we would be in

Hell. So here we are, begging for mercy, hating that we weren't stronger.

I'm leaving. I'll never be back. This place feels like a raging nightmare.

Hertzog exited, hoping he had lost consciousness from a lack of food or the enormous strain of Thomas's death. He tried shaking off the bewildering conversation with Sparky by driving fast. The car's DVD player interrupted his focus, emitting a clicking sound, then starting without a prompt. Scanning the instrument panel for a clue of how the DVD player seemed to begin on its own, Hertzog remembered changing the II Devo music DVD to a favorite audiobook and turning down the volume as he pulled into the parking lot at Sparky's Place. Feeling lame, he allowed the narrator to continue reading Herman Melville's classic, *Moby-Dick*.

Nevertheless, ere long, the warm, warbling persuasiveness of the pleasant, holiday weather we came to, seemed gradually to charm him from his mood.

For, as when the red-cheeked, dancing girls, April and May, trip home to the wintry, misanthropic woods; even the barest, ruggedest, most thunder-cloven old oak will at least send forth some few green sprouts, to welcome such glad-hearted visitants; so Ahab did, in the end, a little respond to the playful allurings of that girlish air.

More than once did he put forth the faint blossom of a look, which, in any other man, would have soon flowered out in a smile.

As if signaling the end of the novel, Alfred's cell phone chimed to indicate an incoming text message. Deaccelerating, he pulled the Mercedes into the dirt-packed driveway of a dairy farm and read the text, then repeated out loud, "From the coroner's office: Cause of death—cardiac arrest."

Putting the phone in its cradle in the center console, he accelerated the car hard, spraying pebbles and dirt while exclaiming loudly, "Thank you, Jesus."

EPILOGUE

To Thomas's surprise, he had been able to gain access to Miss Cartwright's computer, where she stored scientific notes and formulas. He took the data and sold it to an international terrorist ring, unaware it was bogus intel set up to thwart the theft of valuable company assets. Once Thomas had taken the bait, Hertzog alerted the FBI. They headed up an investigation, which led to criminal charges against the terrorist ring for planning human genocide campaigns by using the drug.

As predicted by the F.B.I., it wouldn't take long for Thomas's arrangements with the terrorists to unravel. Finding the formulas worthless, the group pursued Thomas with the intent to assassinate him.

Some experiments go unrecorded. They are never meant to be a part of history. Never meant to be on display for us to have to explain to our children. Instead, they reside in the scientist's mind, protecting both the innocent and the guilty.

Dr. Alfred Hertzog retired not long after he proved the miracle drug's efficiency in saving lives. A short time after retirement, he disappeared, eventually showing up in a small village in the foothills where he bought a ragged vineyard and converted it to a sustainable operation growing Riesling grapes. He named the vineyard after its locale: Blue Heaven Acres.

ROSE GOLD OBSESSION

A-L-L-Y-S-O-N-T-H-O-M-P-S-O-N

Magistrate Judge Steven O'Shaunessy presiding over the district's late afternoon hearing spelled the victim's name for the accomplished stenographer who wore her least comfortable work shoes, black stilettos with a tiny black and yellow bow. The bows matched her crisp mustard-colored pantsuit and black blouse. Angela Portaleski chose her outfits for hearings and court appearances based on the many sports teams she followed. This week it was the NFL Pittsburgh Steelers (black and gold). Next week her outfits would be orange and white with smokey grey accents for the Tennessee Volunteer's men's basketball team. Spinning her head to the left as if it were on a swivel, she acknowledged the Judge's assistance with a quick nod.

When Angela moved her head, those seated at the oversized conference table followed her movement in unison. The collective action allowed Matt, the young man appearing for his hearing, to inspect further the large pendant hanging from her thick pink neck. The pendant resembled an oversized gold-plated pocket watch. Matching earrings in the shape of miniature pocket watches swung as she moved her head to acknowledge the Judge. When engrained in stenography, her body had a slight rhythmic side-to-side bob as if it set the cadence for typing the transcripts. The swaying motion caused the tiny watches to swing methodically, perhaps ticking off the time until she could leave her post.

An imposing six-foot, one hundred ninety pounds, Matt displayed an even temperament during the legal proceedings. The software engineer was considered smart and likable, and the assembled were convinced Matt's action against Allyson Thompson was unintentional.

Judge O'Shaunessy employed an excellent line up of experts to weigh in and support his ruling: the county's chief Coroner, the local police department's homicide investigator, a psychiatrist, a social worker, a junior clerk, and a victim's advocacy specialist. The panel, seated in a beige-colored conference room with brown speckled carpet and wainscoting nicked by years of chairs being pushed against the railing, reviewed records and transcripts of prior proceedings.

The Judge reminded them of Matt's unblemished record, describing it as "Clean as a whistle until the bar scene."

Stone-dead silence matched the graying sky that masked the day's remaining sun as Judge O'Shaunessy declared a recommended sentence "To repair the emotional damage caused by the traumatic events to save the young man." Nodding in agreement to the mittimus, Matt committed to three years of in-patient psychiatric observation and therapy. The legal consignment put a faint smile on his face. Eyeing each expert around the conference table, he lingered at the stenographer-- a success by day and a tramp of costume jewelry by night.

Angela looked up from her stenotype machine, disturbed by Matt's stare. Nervously adjusting the pendant and earrings, she worried the little bow ties were still securely attached to her shoes.

When clubbing on weekends with her friends, Angela's body dripped bling. From dangling earrings to baubles around her neck to an assortment of fake gemstones and knock off diamonds, she spent time and money feeding her obsession. Her showy-like presence ignited the clubs as if an electric plug protruded from her backside. Plug her in, and she dazzled the male patrons. On a few occasions, Matt had seen her and wondered where she worked. He guessed she was in an unfulfilling job; otherwise, why prance around the dance floor showing off accessories. Matt knew how deadly an accessory obsession could be.

The pocket watch, the wall clock, and Matt's heart gonged. Breathing turned into panting as his eyes followed Angela as she left the room. He blinked hard, transforming his eyes into hot pokers to pierce her body. Clasping his hands in front of him as if he were adjusting his suit jacket button, he imagined his hands wringing her neck like a baker kneads bread dough. The forcefulness would tear her skin, choking her but not before expelling a mix of saliva and blood. The panting continued as the guard escorted him to the first floor of the courthouse.

To tamp the vileness of Angela's cruel and daring decision to wear matching accessories, he blamed her obsession on the Judge's heavy-handed dress code. Despite the Judge's calm voice and soft demeanor, his dress code and sentencing were notoriously brutal. If one to three years was suitable for other judges, O'Shaunessy handed down three-to-five-year sentences. Angela's habit of wearing stilettos appeared to push the limitations of the strict guidelines. But Matt learned from his friend Scotty, a lawyer who helped him prepare for the hearings; the Judge ignored Angela wearing stilettos based on both he and his wife's wardrobe during their weekly in-home date nights: black rhinestone dotted stilettos and matching purple silk bathrobes.

THE MEETING

A few weeks before the bar incident, Matt was shopping at a department store in the mall beside his office building during a lunch hour. Making his way to the men's department, he loitered in the jewelry department, eyeing a display of matching pendant and earrings sets. A clerk interrupted his survey asking if he needed help. Matt looked up, scanned the clerk from the neck up for earrings, necklace, a scarf, or headband, then dropped his eyes reading her name tag, *ALLISON*.

"Any sets in rose gold?" he rattled to the small, bouncy brunette. "It's so popular right now. We might have one or two sets left here somewhere," she replied to the hunk dressed in a button-down grey shirt, black pants, and a black leather belt adorned with a silver, rose gold, and copper buckle. She wanted to compliment him on the stylish belt but sensed displeasure in his voice. Matt backed away from the display table and Allison's warmness. A sign at the top of the display read "$21.99 Gift Sets." A grotesquely oversized rose gold circular pendant adorned with clear cut glass meant to look like glittering diamonds sat near the sign. The pendant's pinkness glowed in the customer's savory gaze.

Allison's inability to immediately spot the rose gold set sparked Matt's directive, "Look at the top of the heap," to which she gushed, "Oh yes, good eyes." As she reached for the box, he told her in a breathy tone, "I don't have time now to buy it; let me just look." He took the box, outstretched his arm then held the box close to Allison's neck as if he were holding up a dress to a woman's body. Allison blushed, asking, "How does it look on me?" Matt paused and whispered in a dark tone, "The rose gold highlights your hair."

He winked while handing her the box and walked to the men's department, contemplating how much force he would need to twist her neck, causing vertebrae to pop through her white porcelain skin. The squirming and screeches would announce her plunge into paralysis, causing a near infantile state for the remainder of her shortened existence.

Matt snorted, flung his head back, and rifled through the neatly stacked white t-shirts looking for his size.

BRASS AND WALNUT

In the Brass and Walnut Bar, seated at a bar stool in the corner of her eye, she saw his hand picking up what she thought was an empty beer bottle. Allyson's glance aligned with a grand swing of Matt's arm. He would claim he had no idea how close she was to him. His head never veered when he swung his arms down in one fluid forceful motion.

At the final hearing, Judge O'Shaunessy repeated his initial description of the blow to Allyson Thompson's head as "uncalculated and misfortunate." Dr. Chartwell, the psychiatrist assigned to the case, called Allyson's unfortunate accident "The epitome of having a bad karma day."

Dr. Greene, the County Coroner, described the collision between the force of the rounded thick brown glass bottom of the beer bottle and Allyson's soft, pliable tissue as "A reverberation to the body leading to cardiac arrest instigated by a fresh dose of cocaine. The drug set off electric impulses overloading her heart. The cardiac arrest would have been quite a quick death with a screaming jolt to her chest, literally erupting her heart's valve. If I may use layman's terms, Miss Thompson's body had enough of the toxic chemical to screw up an elephant."

The assemblage concurred with Dr. Greene that Matt's strength and Allyson's small features along with her doped-up state meant there was little pain endured before her body collapsed, dying on the way to the floor. "Less than a second of pain separated life from cardiac arrest that then triggered a massive stroke, and death."

The chief investigator reported, "Revival efforts by EMTs were futile and unnecessary as the victim lost considerable blood and the body was limp upon initial inspection. No pulse and no breath were recorded."

Scotty, Matt's childhood friend, entered the Brass and Walnut, eager to share a few drinks with Matt, and spied him as he suddenly raised his arms then forcefully dropped them. The empty beer bottle he was holding appeared to hit her, knocking her to the ground accidentally.

Scotty first recounted the bar scene to the Judge as the father and son stood in their bass boat on Lake Silver Loch, casting lines into the mist-soaked morning. The Judge insisted his only son join him for weekend trips to the lake. Dutifully Scotty obliged his father, who often shared with Scotty decisions he made about essential family issues.

When Scotty was a senior in college, his LSAT (Law School Admittance Test) scores prevented him from applying to the state university. The Judge made reservations at a Lake Silver Loch, carting his son off to fish and discuss options. The next fall, Scotty was enrolled in law school at a small college near the lake. The Judge often visited Scotty and the law school's dean, a former classmate of Judge O'Shaunessy. "Good to keep up with your law school classmates, Scotty. You never know when you'll need to support one of their pet projects, son. "

On the fishing trip shortly after the bar incident, the Judge shared with Scotty that the court-appointed psychiatrist, Dr. Chartwell, diagnosed Matt with an emotional disorder requiring extensive treatment. "Best thing for the young man is to commit himself to a treatment program for trauma and addiction. He'll get the help he needs to get back to his job. We will need your help, son, to make sure Matt agrees with the treatment plan. You two can stay in contact. Hell, I bet we can arrange for the two of you to take a day here and there to get some fishing in near the hospital. We are optimistic about fixing what's bothering him." The

Judge reminded Scotty, "Miss Thompson was on a path of self-destruction and, at some point, would have experienced cardiac arrest from her cocaine addiction. It's a shame, son. She had a teenager's body with little flesh on those bones to soften the impact and a weakened heart from drug abuse."

BEHAVIOR MATTERS

Matt was wrestled to the grimy floor by two burly customers who thought a fight broke out when the young brunette toppled off the stool. Sitting on a wooden bench outside the holding pen at the police station, Matt crossed his arms to contain the trembling. The palm of his left hand felt the smear of filth on his dress shirt. Upon closer inspection, imperfectly shaped dark spots dotted the shirt sleeve. He sighed, thinking not even a super strength spot remover would erase her blood.

Reality quickly engulfed him. He feared charges of manslaughter. Scrambling to line up his story and build a defense, he chose not to divulge to the investigator or psychiatrist his encounter with Allyson at the department store. It might influence the sentencing.

Both the investigator and the psychiatrist were curious about Matt wildly swinging his arms and holding an empty beer bottle. Dr. Chartwell inquired of Matt several times what prompted the action, but Matt never let on his intent to hurt Allyson. During treatment, Dr. Chartwell asked Matt why he chose to smash the bottle on Allyson's head. Matt deflected the question by sharing he had tapped the empty bottle on the bar before stretching his arms. Like a conductor tapping his baton to quiet an orchestra, he wanted the crowd at the bar to join him in a raucous rendition of Beethoven's 5th Symphony opening.

In a personal battle with drug addiction, Dr. Chartwell empathized with Matt and was determined to get the best treatment possible for the young man. The veteran psychiatrist knew this was a challenging case, zinged by the conductor story and others like it. Near the end of the three years of treatment, Chartwell reported his patient made considerable progress in relieving his mild aversion to "women displaying accessory obsession."'

Further, Chartwell reported, "The third-floor nurses and aides have found the patient approachable, amenable, and often light-hearted. His chattiness, particularly with the female aides about skincare, weight loss, and hairstyles, showed cooperative behavior."

The stellar record carried one blemish, an incident in which Matt quickly recovered thanks to Dr. Chartwell's pharmacological wizardry. "You can't draw an intricate Breitling watch on your wrist with a pen you found on an aide's lunch tray in the T.V. room and expect that we'll not raise it as an issue. And to make matters worse, you had to pen the phrase, *Lust for Rust* on the inside of your other arm like a tattoo? What the hell, Matt?" sneered the psychiatrist. "Do you miss your Breitling that much, or are you just bored out of your mind? Go to your *safe spot* and hang out there for a while until the ink wears off." Matt heard his mother's high-pitched whiney voice in the psychiatrist's scolding, reminding him of an incident when he was ten. He shared the story with Chartwell, hoping he would understand how his mother fashioned his emotional health.

I sat cross-legged on my bed in the late afternoon when my mother abruptly came into my bedroom and caught me playing my X-box instead of doing homework. She screamed, "You freaking geek," ripping the box's cord out of the electric socket then whipped it like a lasso close to my head. The cable missed me, but her wedding ring flew off her finger and bounced on my desk, landing against the base of my reading light. She never retrieved it before she slammed the door, yelling, "Now, you've made dinner late." I never knew why she came into my room. I asked her later, and she shrugged her shoulders like it wasn't necessary.

The ring sat on my desk, sat in silence, unaware of my growing hatred for gold, wedding bands, and marriage. When Mom called me for dinner, I put the ring in my hand and went into the kitchen instead of the dining room. I said, "Here, Mom," opening my fist to reveal the gold band with two tiny diamonds. I thought I saw a little tear in the corner of her eye. She took it and slid it onto her ring finger, then gave it a few twirls, maybe locking it in place. The whole thing made me dizzy. She told me to sit down at the breakfast table chair and take a couple of deep breaths. Stirring the spaghetti sauce, she told me I was overly sensitive. It wasn't the first time she made me feel sick by screaming at me.

CLOSE ENCOUNTERS

Three years after the hearing, Judge O'Shaunessy released Matt, confident he was okay. However, he tethered him to the county's health and human services division by ordering him to attend Alcoholics Anonymous (A.A.) meetings and check-in monthly with a social worker.

His first A.A. meeting was in a brightly decorated classroom in the local Baptist church's basement. Chrissy, an effervescent young woman, introduced herself, and the two struck up a conversation. Each week she made Matt feel comfortable and light-hearted by swooning over the décor, pointing out the cute construction paper animals pinned to the bulletin board, or pointing out the Ten Commandments written on the blackboard. "Not exactly set in stone, those rules," she joked.

Not permitted to date other A.A. members, they decided to build an enduring friendship by meeting up for coffee or a movie or a bike ride. Chrissy helped fill in for Matt what he had missed in the past three years, often referencing articles in "People" magazine or movies on Netflix.

On this Saturday morning, Chrissy coerced Matt into accompanying her on a shopping trip even though his demeanor was still a bit raw. He wasn't sure if an occasional upset stomach was due to a change in diet or inability to find a job.

Early in his treatment, Dr. Chartwell showed Matt how to redirect thoughts and actions by going to a "safe spot" that was calming and peaceful. It took Matt thirty seconds to identify the spot -- a flat island lapped by small waves where bonefish lived in the brilliant turquoise water. Belize's waters were calming. Matt had become quite adept at using his "safe spot" when things started to crumble.

Matt and Chrissy turned the corner toward the Tiffany store; Matt cursed Chrissy while looking down the street to the store's front windows as he felt mushy thinking about entering an evil sanctuary that might be full of women with accessory obsession. He was fearful spending time in the store might undo the little progress he had made.

"C'mon, Matt. It's fun even if all we can do is look," gushed Chrissy, and Matt pulled open the oversized brass door to the hellish chamber. Tip-toeing over the threshold, Chrissy sensed his hesitation and pointed to the chairs on the far side of the store for "impatient men."

Matt felt like a mad animal in a cage. He panted and went to his "safe spot," combined with a few deep breaths. Without completely losing control, he looked around for another diversion spotting a square plexiglass display in the middle of the store. Two Tiffany designed table tennis paddles were on display. He quickly excused himself from Chrissy's cooing over earring sets to study the exquisitely polished mahogany-handled paddles with Tiffany blue leather palms. The paddles held a chunky gold necklace adorned by a gold plate ping pong ball charm. He tried to erase the chain and charm in his mind's eye, but the spotlight on the display case made them shine in his eyes, igniting the desirous thought of how he so wanted to slice Allyson's tiny wrist holding the gold bracelet she wore to the Brass and Walnut Bar.

A clerk interrupted his curious stare into the plexiglass box. A voluptuous woman with bronze skin, brown eyes, and beautiful black curly hair stood beside him in admiration of the display, and Matt and inquired, "You play table tennis? It would help if you had these!" Matt nodded as he looked into her magnetic eyes, radiating a peculiar peacefulness. His jaw softened, replying, "Unfortunately, I've played a lot of ping pong recently. I guess that's what attracted me to the display." He glanced at the clerk's name tag, *STELLA.*

Stella shared with Matt that most men were fascinated by the paddles, never inquiring about the necklace's price. Stella looked across the store at the manager who was helping Chrissy with a sparkling necklace.

"There's a chair over there, Matt, when you get tired," Stella told Matt. Looking at her with surprise, Matt asked the clerk how she knew his name. "Oh, I heard your friend say it when you came in." Matt didn't recall Chrissy using his name while conversing over the earrings but thought it too obscure to pursue.

Stella walked away, stating, "If there is anything you want to look at, let me know." Taking himself "impatient straight back chairs with silver molded arms," he sat down in a heap disgusted to be sitting in a lair's den of jewelry. He wondered how long he would last before having to leave to avoid a violent outburst. At least, he thought, Stella isn't decked out with some oversized rose gold brooch and a clunky bracelet to accent her fuchsia dress.

He didn't know where to look, so he locked his eyes on the table tennis display. Stella walked his way, asking if he wanted a cup of mineral water. Before he could decline, she put her finger up as if to stop him from speaking, bent over slightly, and put her face close to his, whispering, "Do you remember Carissa Maria from Belize?" The question pierced Matt's heart like an arrow. His eyes danced wildly, and his jaw dropped. He struggled to speak. "Of course. Why do you ask?"

"Turns out," said Stella sporting a big smile and pulling back from the young man, "Carissa Maria is my cousin and has been asking about you since your release." The remark made Mark blush and remark, "Oh, so that's how you knew my name." "Right, right, "replied Stella. "And to boot, get this, I'm a friend of Chrissy's. We arranged for you to be here so I could give you Carissa's new phone number, just in case." Wanting to kiss Stella, Matt also felt a strange sense of wanting to strangle Chrissy.

Stella texted the number while Matt was still caught up in the thought of Carissa Maria. "I guess Chrissy gave you my cell phone number, eh?" he inquired.

"Yea, Matt. We've been planning this for weeks." Matt quizzed Stella, "And Carissa Maria still wants to talk to me?"

"Worried sick about you since she heard you were in prison."

"Okay, Stella, technically, I wasn't imprisoned."

Stella smiled, replying, "Sorry. How you say it, Matt, an insane asylum?" Matt huffed back, "It was rehab. Just call it rehab, Stella."

Chrissy, donning a diamond-studded overlay necklace, pranced over to the two of her best friends, "Isn't it just marvelous?" Matt replied in his smoothest Bogart voice, "Darling, it's stunning. And the price tag is too." Chrissy sharply turned around to make her way to the counter and disrobe the necklace.

His new cell phone vibrated from the inner pocket of the old tweed jacket. The phone number looked odd until he remembered 5-0-1 was the country code for Belize. Looking at Stella, she shrugged her shoulders, saying to Matt, "I guess she beat you to it, Matt." Unveiling the text message while getting up from the chair, he read it in her sweet voice, "Hiya Mattie. This is my new phone number. Luv to hear from U."

Raising his voice so Chrissy could hear him across the store without disturbing the other customer Matt declared he was going outside. The store's heavy brass door opened automatically as if they a gate releasing him from prison. A beam of sunlight caused him to shield his eyes to re-read the text message.

Matt didn't bother rehearsing what to say. He didn't give himself time to formulate answers to the obvious questions or explain what made him commit to three years of treatment. "I'm a fool," he thought as he placed the call.

"Hello," came across clearly. Closing his eyes, he savored the two simple syllables that took a deep dive into his complicated heart. Carissa Maria immediately took him to her private estate where peace reigned, softness draped the walls like snug-fitting wallpaper, and they soaked in their pools of conversations. She never led him to a demonic state. Instead, Carissa Maria nudged him along nature's path, pointing out native flowers, insects, and shells' distinctive patterns. She shared crevices hiding treasures: a leaf with yellow lines, a feather from a gull that was black on one side and white on the other, a wasp nest with delicate niches and paper-thin seams. It was an explorer's dream.

Dr. Chartwell reminded Matt of the women he identified as being afflicted by accessory obsession were characteristically weak souls. The strong, he explained, could prevent obsessions. Clarissa Maria was the strongest woman Matt knew—dignified, somewhat shy, and deeply spiritual despite being a prostitute.

Carissa Maria shared with Stella the love she felt for Matt and the predicament of seeing him only once a year. How to tell him she was in love with him when she needed all the other men who visited the island to survive? Matt's former co-worker who visited Belize last year with buddies told Carissa Maria of the Brass and Walnut Bar incident. She was relieved Matt was in rehab but worried his technology skills would diminish while institutionalized. If she could speak to him, she could share her desire to be with him. Maybe, she could help him heal. And perhaps they could share life in Belize.

The phone conversation lasted less than two minutes before Chrissy flung open the doors, turned to her right to see Matt on the phone standing about ten feet away. She rushed to him and squeezed his arm. Not knowing Matt was talking to Carissa Maria, she tugged at the jacket, "Hang up, Matt, I'm hungry. All the jewelry made me ravished." He ended the conversation with Carissa Maria in mid-sentence, promising to call her again that night. She replied she preferred a call back in the morning.

"Let's get a burger, Matt," Chrissy exclaimed, taking his arm and leading him in the direction of the trendy Allure Café while opening her purse to extract a Pall Mall cigarette. "Come along, Mattie. It's a beautiful day for Tiffany jewelry and a burger. You should have a Cuban cigar for being so patient and for not being disturbed that Stella and I set up again with Clarissa Maria!"

Matt touched his shirt pocket where the thin Cuban cigar-shaped like a black pencil was stowed. "It's so rich and flavorful, Chrissy; I think I'll save it for after lunch," he said, inhaling the smoke from Chrissy's cigarette. The smoke gave him a slight rush before he closed his eyes, only to see a cement block swinging precariously past his face. Abruptly tightening his grip on Chrissy's wrist and throwing back his head, the image scared him, catapulting him to the Brass and Walnut where he heard the screams, witnessed the chaos, mesmerized by Allyson's bloodied swollen face. He looked down at the sidewalk as it fluttered and pulled Chrissy close to him, steadying himself, desperately trying to get to his "safe spot."

Chrissy held him close, slowed her pace, and asked Matt if he wanted to talk about what happened at Tiffany's. He managed to mumble a "No" while recovering from the cruel flashback.

After lunch, he retrieved the beloved skinny cigar from his pocket savoring its delight and the high it gave him. It mimicked the split second in which he felt a Superman-like power rip through his body, aiming the base of the beer bottle at Allyson's head, hoping to shatter the dangling gold earring and the diamond stud decorating her ear lobe. The shards were meant to pierce her brain, slicing her obsession into slivers so the devil could distribute them to the burning souls in Purgatory. It would be a test—would they embrace the bloodied tissue, devouring it, or would they spit it out and yell it was poisoned flesh from a sinner?

Matt often envisioned his afterlife. Facing his creator, he would regret not seeking help before the aversion to women with an accessory obsession turned violent.

HERE I AM

The monthly non-denominational church services in the dining hall at the mental health and rehabilitation facility provided Matt with some solace. The aides readied the room for the late afternoon service clearing the orange-colored sturdy plastic trays, wiping down the lunch tables, tidying the wooden chairs, and spraying Renuzit to dismiss lingering odors from lunch. Inevitably the preachers started late awaiting the stragglers. An older aide urged the residents to attend, "Get yourself in there. It's good for your soul like your Momma's chicken soup!"

The service included Bible verses, hymns played by a guitarist, sometimes accompanied by a clarinet player dressed in a crisp white long-sleeved shirt, black pants, and colorful bow tie. (The residents childishly commented on the bowtie instead of listening to the readings.) Church wrapped up with a reminder to be kind to one another and be open to the healing process to erase desperation. But desperation was a commonality that never went away. As helpful as they tried to be with one another, it was the desperate helping the desperate.

The clergymen cleared their throats, signaling the start of the final hymn. The musicians began a rendition of *Here I Am, Lord,* just as two patients started to fuss at each other about a chair inadvertently moved toward the aisle. The aide quickly moved the chair to make room for a patient using his walker to maneuver his way toward the hallway.

Yelling voices and scraping chair legs on the wooden floor overtook the singing. Making a cocoon by crossing his arms and legs, Matt dropped his head into his shoulders, hoping to silence the chaos and the tremors. A tear stung his eye as he struggled to hear the second and third verse above the escalating argument. Albert, a young patient, seeking help from multiple suicide attempts, became annoyed at the confusion and jumped up from his chair, causing it to skid several feet while announcing, "I'm done with this crap." The declaration brought a few outbursts, including, "Geez, Albert, you're in church." Matt spun around in his chair, looking down the hallway to the nurse's station, hoping the nurse would be there to diffuse the situation. Albert made his way to the back of the room, flapping his arms and screeching like a large bird about to take flight.

At the next counseling session with Dr. Chartwell, Matt shared Albert's unruly remark and behavior, tartly asking, "Is there no respect among the prisoners, Doc?" Dr. Chartwell looked down at his notepad then raised it, covering his mouth and nose like a football coach calling out a play to the quarterback during a time out on the field. When he lowered the white-lined pad, his face carried a stern stare. "Believe me, Matt. This is no prison." Matt's face turned red, embarrassed by his sarcastic comment and shamed by the doctor's reminder he had been saved from incarceration for his violent act at the Brass and Walnut.

Stifling a growl, he wanted to smear Allyson's blood on Matt so he could smell the distinct copper-like aroma. He turned the white Bic pen over in his hand, staring at Matt's throat, gritting his teeth. Hesitant to disturb Matt, he carefully chose his words, whispering, "The photographs of her bloodied body, the shattered skull with her eye grossly embedded..." He stopped abruptly, knowing he should not continue. Swallowing hard, the urge to pierce Matt's throat with the pen, plunging it repeatedly until his squeals turned into gasps for air and his eyes rolled back in his head, evaporated.

Staring at the pathetic young man with an incurable addiction to women's accessories and a poorly calibrated moral compass, Chartwell felt frustrated and angered by the inability to change Matt's behavior. The young man was distraught as well, sneering at the psychiatrist, "I won't forget what I was given."

TAKING FLIGHT

The re-introduction to society felt like a long inhale on an Opus X cigar. The social worker and psychiatrist agreed the bonefishing trip would be a perfect balm. Packing most of his clothes for the travel left few possessions. Clothes, electronics, and his car were sold to cover expenses while institutionalized. The last phase of the rehabilitation cost $40,000. His parents cashed in their IRAs instead of opting for a high-interest payment plan. Matt felt horrible for their financial plight but told his Dad the trip wasn't frivolous. It offered a new beginning, especially if he could avoid bars like the Brass and Walnut with diamond-studded skimpy babes swaying their bobbles in his face.

Today he would record the new start in a journal given to him by the aides. Would the first entry be short and sweet like the peck on his mother's? Or would it be written with gusto like the first kiss he and Clarisa Maria would share?

Leaving the house and heading down the sidewalk to his Lyft ride, Matt's Dad caught up to him, pressing a paperback-sized plastic case into his hand. "Open it, Matt," his father urged. Matt unclipped the light blue box. Inside was an eclectic collection of colorful fly-fishing flies. The gift overwhelmed him, and he could barely thank his Dad, who told him the guys at the Ole Fly Shop handpicked the flies for use in Belize. Matt looked beyond the man's frayed silver hair to the white vinyl-sided house with the tired and muted red aluminum shutters, then turned again, this time catching a glimpse of his mother silhouetted in the home's glass storm door.

Settled in the passenger seat of the four-door silver Honda Civic, he unzipped his knapsack and tucked the plastic box between his journal and baseball cap, making a mental note to transfer the case into his checked luggage. He chuckled, thinking of how the pack of fly-fishing ties made to look like small crabs might set off alarms at the airport. At yesterday's session with his social worker, she reminded him to pack anything suspicious or questionable in his checked-in luggage. "The less stress, the more room for healing," she stated matter-of-factly. Matt hugged the knapsack begging God to heal him.

As the car rambled through the neighborhood on the way to the expressway, Matt recalled Dr. Chartwell telling him healing would happen when he trained his mind to ignore bling. "Just like you train your brain on a diet by not replacing the doughnut with a low carb slice of bread, you turn your brain off to even contemplating food. When you get to the point where you can look at a diamond pendant on a woman's neck, and it means nothing to you; you stop listening to the chatter; stop trying to read her mind; stop caring about her body language—you're making progress."

Matt turned and looked at the twenty-something Lyft driver, Stevie Holden. Scanning her for bling made her look over at the curious passenger, but she quickly looked again at the road. Silently Matt asked Stevie, "Do I see nothing, or is there nothing to see?" To his surprise, a voice emanated from the car radio's speakers answering, *you'll know, know, know.* Nodding back to the late Amy Winehouse, Matt told himself, *so I will, will, will.*

The Cessna 208B Caravan flight to Belize City gave passengers a unique view of the green and brown freckled islands dotting the ocean's blue hues. The constant ticking sound of the propellers mesmerized him, putting Matt into a trance. Gingerly he opened the door to his soul and cautiously entered the cavernous abode of his being. The room, dotted with a few friends and acquaintances, ignited in chatter as he closed the heavy iron door with a small window with bars.

Scotty crept out from behind the door, pleading, "Don't blow it, buddy."

Dr. Chartwell, dressed in nothing but short running shorts and shoes, stopped abruptly exclaiming, "Feeling desperate? Get help."

Matt's Dad standing off to the side as if he were at a youth soccer game, clapped and pumped his fists, "Good for you for not giving in."

Chrissy merrily skipped by yelling, "I can't wait to visit you in Belize!"

The social worker riding by on her bicycle pointed at Matt, "Don't experiment with any drugs."

His former boss zipped by on a Razor scooter, almost clipping Matt, "No recommendation for you. It's against the policy."

Allyson briskly walked toward Matt, stopped, pulled her hair back, revealing pearl and topaz stud earrings. "Look what I just bought on Jet-TV."

Looking around the room for others, he turned to face the door sternly, telling himself three times with increasing emphasis, "Get to your safe place."

After visiting the messy, chaotic canyon of his soul, the mocking remarks made him sad. Other times when he would drift to his inner self, it was a softer, forgiving state. The rawness was not entirely unexpected. His soul, shaken from leaving home, institutional living, and heaps of mind-altering drugs, were bound to lessen his self-respect and self-love. Despite a "team surrounding the team," he left the institution and rehabilitation unit drained and still obsessively cruel to women who wore rose gold jewelry. Looking around the half-empty plane, he focused on what lay ahead: Belize, bonefish, and Carissa Maria. Trying to make light of the seriousness of his mental state, he asked, "So what if I'm an obsessed maniac?" answering himself, "If I keep to myself, I am harmless. Most men have some hang-ups with women. If they aren't bothered by them, they should be."

His thoughts softened as he looked at the seatback in front of him and saw Carissa Maria, naked, sweating, and smiling. She had dropped her shoulders and raised her head, and she was delectable. The magical mirage was abruptly interrupted when the young woman, three rows in front, turned her head toward him and peered between the seats. She caught Matt's attention as they boarded the plane even though Matt rushed past but paused for a quick scan of her body for earrings, a necklace, a watch, bracelets, or rings. He leaned into the aisle to get a better view as she slowly turned her head, peering out the window across the row of seats. Flicking her long straight blond hair revealed four-diamond stud earrings. "One for each of the long, lusty lovers," snickered Matt. He closed his eyes tightly, squinting, and rubbed his forehead to lock the door of evil voices. He kept his eyes closed while successfully muffling the rapping of Satan's knocking on the door of his soul. A breeze swirled at his feet.

The draft tickled his sockless feet. Bending over to inspect his Oxford loafers and ankles, a moan smacked him in the cheek then spit in his eye. He pulled away, swatting at his ankles as if mosquitos were swarming. "Damn moaning." he exclaimed, "Leave me alone!"

Sometimes the moan would play in his head ten or twenty times a day. It was the last sound Allyson made as she bounced from bar stool to cement floor to death.

The years of replaying the low guttural moan chipped away at his sanity. To gain composure, Matt recited the Coroner's remark at his hearing, "Less than a second of pain separated life from cardiac arrest that then triggered a massive stroke and death."

Scoffing at the remark, Matt wanted to tell Dr. Greene he was wrong. Allyson didn't die in a second. The Coroner needed to know about the long guttural moan.

One day over coffee, Matt would tell Dr. Greene about the long moan. But being beaten up for so many years by so many horrible situations and emotions, he would bluntly tell Matt how he changed the report to save him from prison. Matt would scoff at the notion. Dr. Greene would produce the original Coroner's account. In a deliberate tone, he would read how the violent blow to her temple imploded the brain, causing convulsion, how the jawbone impaled her throat, and the eye socket sunk into a pool of blood. He would slowly read of the body's blinding pain and last futile gasps for air.

The young man would have no retort except to write it off as "Imaginary and contrived," to which Dr. Greene would reply as he leaned close to Matt, "Nothing worth learning from is an image."

Matt's thin pink lips formed a casual but somewhat sly smile. He knew he and the Coroner would never share that cup of coffee nor the conversation. Disappointingly, he would never get to share Allyson's guttural moan he had practiced to perfection.

Opening his eyes, he was relieved to be seated in the plane and not on the barstool drinking his second Rusty Nail before guzzling a bottle of imported beer. As if the pilots were part of the trance, the plane made a blunt bank toward Belize City Airport. The cabin creaked, and the small dog seated by blonde three rows away whimpered. Matt swallowed hard to pop his ears, stating, "What the hell?" He could see the landing gear (permanently in place) and noted the tires' small size from his seat. Deciding the pilots were probably avoiding a popup cloud, he focused on meeting his friend and cabbie, Manuel, a healer and a giant of a man. Nervously, he pondered how to tell him what had transpired since the last fishing trip to the majestic barrier reef's prolific flats.

Deplaning to the tarmac, a Chihuahua bounded toward him, dragging its leash. The dog's owner, the young blonde woman seated in front of Matt, caught up to the dog as Matt grabbed the leash. "Oh, sorry. Petunia got away. Looks like she's making a new friend!" Matt smiled, spotting a copper bracelet dotted with black onyx pieces on the dog's owner's wrist. Petunia and Matt both panted. Matt gave the leash to the woman, nodded, adjusted his sunglasses, and turned away.

His steely blue eyes were backlit in neon red, reflecting the flames of Hell where imprisoned souls pulled the chunky black steel prison bars pleading with Satan to be removed from the fiery flames searing their bare feet. But Satan reminded them what hellish lives they led on earth, spending hours choosing accessories to adorn their bodies. He wanted to grab the blond woman's hair, shake her violently while hissing, "What makes accessory obsessed women like you think dogs are more like humans than the rotting homeless people you walk over in the street? It makes me crazy."

How many times had he used the phrase during group therapy sessions? Young interns and aides found Matt's calculated usage of "It makes me crazy" amusing. Some of the not so drug-induced patients would look at him with skepticism. Dr. Chartwell eventually reprimanded Matt. He chose to share with Matt how first responders at the Brass and Walnut spoke of Matt's work as an "overt act of violence." Chartwell reminded Matt, "It took a lot of convincing to get you committed instead of convicted. If you ever wanted to be on stage conducting a symphony with a full house of harsh critics, that was it, Matt. "

With his luggage in hand, Matt scanned the lineup of cabs, spied his faithful friend, Manuel, and trotted the last few feet to his vehicle. The two embraced, shared a few laughs, and piled into the shiny red Mercury Montego convertible.

Manuel was introduced to the lush island years ago when he escorted church youth groups on mission trips to aid the homeless. Impressed by the island's beauty, he was also disturbed by the widespread drug use and crime. He pointed out the issues to the youth group, who shrugged it off as third world problems. The teens were more interested in beach time, swapping t-shirts with other youth group members, and taking photos of the natives.

The last mission trip served as a reward for the teens who had just won the city-wide church youth league Esports championship. Developing a league had been an easier task than Manuel anticipated. The teens embraced the team concept and eagerly competed against other churches for the first-place trophy. The club attracted teens to the gaming center Manuel set up in the church's basement. He'd found a successful way to spread keep teenagers interested in the church now known for its competitive co-ed eSports team, *The Tablets*.

But all the praise heaped high for Manuel's Esports league was upended by a 200-word op-ed (opinion editorial) published in a Sunday edition of the town's daily paper, *The Herald.* The op-ed put a screeching halt to the league. Written by an official from a local reformed church, the gaming league was described as a "vile and putrid" symbol of disturbed youth. "Father Manuel has impregnated our youth with games of violence, killing, and murderous acts. Why is this permitted to flourish?"

Four years ago, when Manuel recounted Matt's incident while ferrying him from the airport to the cigar shop, he expressed deep disappointment in his superior's response. Appalled when he heard the story, Matt offered a paltry response, "Rest reassured Manuel, God forgives those who sin and those who think they have sinned." Manuel shook his head, not looking over to Matt as tears welled in his dark eyes. The memories of the de-frocking, the forced dismissal, and the loss of his church still stung him like nasty wasps. Calming his emotions, he tried to justify his actions for the hundredth time, "I wasn't possessed by anything but the wholesomeness of trying to keep young men and women in decaying churches. And for that, I will burn in Hell."

Silenced by the remark, Matt decided a light-hearted comment might be appreciated. "St. Peter will be so happy to see you at the gates, Manuel. I hear the gamers in Heaven need a new coach." Manuel managed to flash a small smile, "Yea, I also heard St. Augustine is retiring soon. He said St. Paul's team was too hard to control in the playoffs."

Manuel often thought of Matt's words, thanking God for sending a lowly disciple to heal a priest.

Pulling away from the tarmac and gunning the Montego ever so slightly, the cabbie was anxious to converse with his friend, who was equally eager for time with Father Manuel. "Is this just like old times, friend? Are we making the usual stops, the cigar shop, then Carissa Maria's apartment?" Matt nodded, "Yes, sir. Some things never change."

After a four-year absence, Manuel was happy to be reunited with his friend and eager to get caught up. Glancing at Matt as the young man dipped his head, made the sign of the cross with his hand, and spoke slowly, "Bless me, Father, for I have sinned. It has been a little over four years since my last confession."

RESOURCES

2030 UN (United Nations) Agenda for Sustainable Development
https://sdgs.un.org/goals

National Suicide Prevention Hotline
https://suicidepreventionlifeline.org/

National Center for PTSD
https://www.ptsd.va.gov/gethelp/crisis_help.asp

COCKTAIL PAIRINGS

For your enjoyment, you may want to pair these drinks with the Thrillogy short stories. The recipes, based on traditional libations, were modified a bit. After all, according to Lord Penfield in 1867,

In the grand and disorderly pursuit of life, perfection is ill-advised except in the case of cocktails.

WILD LENSES

A Thrillogy is not complete without a signature pairing of a simple yet sustaining drink. The foundation of "Wild Lenses" is a half cup of tea brewed then cooled to room temperature. If you are not a tea drinker, don't worry, the taste does not overwhelm you. Tea is used to expand the other ingredients, not block them. Thus the foundational tea is behind the scenes letting the coconut cream balance the Wild Turkey and the rum.

Serve this drink frozen or on the rocks. If you recall, in the short reads, all the main characters see things that others do not. This drink lights up the senses. It tastes and feels creamy and deep, smells sweet and rooty, and looks dense. The sound of the blender or the shaker awakens the palette.

1 jigger Wild Turkey
½ cup coconut cream
1 jigger Rum (light or dark)
½ cup brewed tea

Blend with ice. Add a dash of hot sauce or a dollop of ice cream. Enjoy!

GAME ON

This drink has an intricate taste that tickles and delights the palette. If you are new to Pimm's, you are in for a treat! Campari Bitters is an iconic aperitive that adds a brilliant ambrosia look. Let the games begin.

1 oz. Gin
1 oz. Pimm's
1 oz. Campari Bitters or Peychaud's Aromatic Cocktail Bitters
Club soda
Slice of orange or cucumber

Place ice in a tall glass, pour in the Gin and Pimm's, then club soda. Top with the Campari Bitters. Gently mix as it does not take much to release the herbal tones and the red coloring. Add a slice of orange or cucumber.

CROWNING SANGRIA

2 oz. Ketel One Grapefruit + Rose Botanicals
3 oz. Chardonnay
3 oz. Orange juice
1 oz. Triple Sec
Fresh Basil for garnish

Splash of sparkling wine (Champagne works well!)

Let the ingredients soak overnight. Strain the Sangria over ice in a tall glass. Garnish with fresh basil and a splash of sparkling wine.

PEARLY BARLEY WATER (as served at Wimbledon and used by athletes as a recovery drink)

½ cup Pearl Barley
4 c. Spring water
3 T. sugar
Juice of one lime
Lemon slices

Mix thoroughly and serve cold with garnishes of lemon!

BLUE REVV

This bright blue colored drink starts as a traditional martini but quickly shows another side when infused with contemporary St. Germain Elderflower liquor (essences of herbal and floral undertones). The toppings make it lighthearted.

1 ½ oz. Vodka
1 oz. Blue Curacao
½ oz. St. Germain Elderflower
Maraschino cherry or plump blueberry soaked in Sweet Vermouth.
Twist of lemon
Splash of grapefruit-flavored carbonated water, if desired.

Soak fruits overnight in Sweet Vermouth. Mix the liquors over ice with vigor, allowing the drink to chill before pouring it in a martini glass or highball glass. Garnish with a Maraschino cherry or a plump blueberry, preferably on a spear or toothpick. To rev up the taste buds, add the smallest twist of lemon.

Note: Vermouth is an aromatized wine and is the French pronunciation for the German word for wormwood, "wermut." Known scientifically as *artemisia absinthium*.

GOLD FURNACE

1 oz. Gold Jagermeister Cinnamon Schnapps
A splash of Tabasco sauce

Tamp the flames with a glass of chilled water.

GOLDEN HOUR

If you know the "Golden Hour" at dawn and dusk, you know it is a favorite of cinematographers and photographers and those wanting to start or end their day on the flats fishing for bonefish. Creamy, dreamy, sturdy, and sweet, it glows.

2 jiggers Seagram's VO Gold
1 jigger Coco Lopez
¼ cup cherry or cranberry juice
Splash of Dry Vermouth
Splash of Ginger Ale
Slice of orange

Mix the liquors gently over shaved ice and strain into a high glass. Mix in the Ginger Ale, top with a splash of Dry Vermouth, and garnish with an orange slice.

CHARTED

The Diplomat drink (dreamt up in 1922) is a complex melody of sweet, dry, smooth, tart flavors supported by an earthy undertone. It is surprisingly refreshing, especially when sipped, allowing the chunk of ice to continue to keep it chilled and controlled.

1.5 oz. Dry Vermouth
¾ oz. Sweet Vermouth
2 dashes Luxardo Maraschino Liquor
Lemon peel with juice intact

Mix all but the Maraschino liquor. Strain into a highball glass containing a large ice cube, preferably a "round cube." Garnish with Luxardo Maraschino and lemon.

CLEANSER

Everyone needs a little brightness to lighten the load. This delicious and refreshing water-based drink is the perfect way to feel energized and cheery.

Mineral Water
Cucumber, thinly sliced
Lime, quartered
Spring mint
Basil (few leaves)
Splash of Grenadine

Chill the liquids for two hours. Strain and pour into a large tumbler and top with Grenadine. Sip slowly to savor the goodness.

ALICE'S RED QUEEN

The drink has nothing to do with the classic book *Alice in Wonderland* but everything to do with celebrating Gin's exquisite taste accentuated with elderberry and topped with cranberry. The lemon compliments the citrus that some say exists in the drink's deep tones in its neat form.

1/2 cup of cranberry juice
1 jigger of Hendricks Gin
½ jigger of St. Germaine Elderflower liqueur
Juice from half a lemon

In a cocktail shaker, add all the ingredients (except fresh cranberries) and plenty of ice, shaking it until frost forms on the shaker. Pour into a chilled martini or coupe glass and dress it up with a few fresh cranberries, either floating or speared. It's a beautiful and tasty drink!